MEMILY

Written by Stephen Cosgrove
Illustrated by Robin James

PRICE STERN SLOAN
Los Angeles

The Serendipity™ series was created by
Stephen Cosgrove and Robin James.

Copyright © 1987, 1994 by Price Stern Sloan, Inc.

Published by Price Stern Sloan, Inc.
A member of The Putnam & Grosset Group,
New York, New York.

Book ISBN: 0-8431-3792-4

10 9 8 7 6 5 4 3 2 1

Dedicated to the one and only Emily, pronounced Memily... one of a kind in a land of duplication.

Stephen

There was a land; a marvelous, green, sweet-smelling land called the Jasmine Jungle, a land brimming with all the mysteries of life and filled with the raucous sounds of all the creatures who lived within. It was here that baby leopards leaped. It was here that elephants of all sizes spritzed and sprayed the jungle with a fine watery mist, causing rainbows to dance from sunbeam to sunbeam. This was the magical Jasmine Jungle.

In the middle of this land there was a meadow. And in this fragrant meadow a small knobby-kneed giraffe, named Memily, was born. Normally, this would not have been such a special event, but until Memily was born there were only two other giraffes in the jungle: Memily's father and, of course, Memily's mother. All the other creatures of the jungle gathered around and "oohhed" and "ahhed" at the newborn baby.

Memily spent the first few weeks of life in the Jasmine Jungle awkwardly learning how to walk. As we all know, giraffes have long lanky legs, and Memily was no exception. It took her a long time to learn to walk on legs so long. She would wobble about the meadow bouncing off a tree here and a bush there as she struggled to gain her balance.

Memily had a problem of sorts. She knew that she was a giraffe, there was no problem with that. She knew about all the dangers of the jungle, for her mother had taught her well. Memily's problem was that she didn't have anybody to play with who was her own size.

One day she joined some bunnies playing a silly forest game. She thought to herself, "What fun! I just love to play tag." Soon a bunny tagged her "it," and she was off chasing the little creatures all over the meadow.

Memily felt just like a bunny— only a lot taller.

The game started innocently, then ended in disaster. One minute, Memily was chasing the bunnies, and the next minute she tripped on a root that the others had jumped over. She flipped; she flopped; and she landed in a heap right on top of all the little bunnies.

One by one, the bunnies popped out of this jungle jumble, until the only one left in the pile of confusion was Memily.

"Gee whiz, Memily!" the bunnies cried. "You could have hurt us that way! You have got to play with someone your own size!"

With that, the bunnies hopped away, leaving Memily tangled and confused. "Well," she thought, "I'll just have to find someone taller to play with."

She struggled to her feet and galloped clumsily on her way, in search of new friends and new games.

Now Memily's only problem with finding someone her own size was the fact that Memily was still growing. Day by day she was growing taller and taller. She tried to play with the lions, but they were too short and much too rough. She tried to play with the monkeys, but Memily had trouble walking on the ground, let alone climbing the trees.

Finally, Memily befriended two zebras and an elephant who were playing a rousing game of hide-and-go-seek. They had no objections to letting Memily play. For, as you know, the more the merrier when you are playing hide-and-go-seek.

One of the zebras counted as the others hid. The elephant hid in the river, with only his trunk sticking out. The other zebra hid in the bush where her stripes disguised her.

Memily dashed around looking for somewhere to hide. She tried to hide with the elephant, but she didn't have a trunk to breathe through. She tried to hide with the zebra, but her neck stuck way out.

Finally, she found a place—at least she thought she was hiding. But when the zebra finished counting he instantly spied Memily behind a pile of rocks. Just where could a tall giraffe hide?

She hid here. She hid there. But her gangly legs or her long neck always stuck out.

Finally, the other animals said, "It's not going to work, Memily! You are just too tall. You have to find someone your own size." Giggling, the three of them dashed into the Jasmine Jungle, leaving Memily with no one to play with.

She looked and looked for someone her own size, but she could find no one. Soon Memily stopped trying to play with the other creatures of the jungle.

Week after week Memily grew and grew, and she became sadder and sadder. She was embarrassed by her height. Whenever any of the other creatures walked by she would turn her head, knowing that they had to look up just to look her in the eye.

And still Memily grew. She began to bow her neck and bend her knees, trying to make herself shorter. Everything she tried was to no avail, for no matter how much she bowed her neck or bent her knees, she was still very tall indeed.

Memily was so embarrassed about being tall that she spent all day hiding amidst the trees that grew at the edge of the jungle. She would stand for hours, munching on sweet leaves and twitching her ears so that the birds wouldn't build a nest on her head.

But the birds would come anyway, twittering and giggling and singing a silly song,

> "Who can you see…
> Taller than a tree?
> It's Memily…. It's Memily!"

Memily would shake her head and the birds would fly away laughing.

One day, as Memily was rustling through the uppermost branches of a very tall tree, she was shocked nearly out of her wits by a head looking back at her from another tree. She looked once, she looked twice, and sure enough there was another creature just as tall as she.

"Hello, there," she said shyly. "Do you have to hide in the trees, too?"

The giraffe laughed and walked over gracefully. "I am not hiding. I am eating the sweet leaves that only grow at the very top. I'm Herschel. Who are you?"

"Memily," she said walking with her knees all bent and her neck bowed.

Herschel laughed. "Why are you walking like that?"

"I have to," said Memily. "Or else I would be taller than the other creatures."

"But you are supposed to be taller," said Herschel. "Some creatures are tall, some are small, but all have their place in the magical Jasmine Jungle."

In time, Memily learned that in nature all creatures are special in their own way.

SHORT IS SHORT,
AND TALL IS TALL.
YOU ARE WHAT YOU ARE,
AND THAT IS ALL!